Alfred's
INSTRUMENTAL
mp3 CD
PLAY-ALONG

Ultimate
Pop & Rock
Instrumental Solos

**Arranged by Bill Galliford, Ethan Neuburg, and Tod Edmondson
Recordings produced by Dan Warner, Doug Emery, and Lee Levin.**

© 2012 Alfred Music
All Rights Reserved

ISBN-10: 0-7390-9496-3
ISBN-13: 978-0-7390-9496-9

Alfred

CONTENTS

25 OR 6 TO 4

Track 2: Demo
Track 3: Play-Along

Words and Music by
ROBERT LAMM

21 GUNS

Words and Music by
BILLIE JOE, GREEN DAY,
DAVID BOWIE and JOHN PHILLIPS

21 Guns - 2 - 1

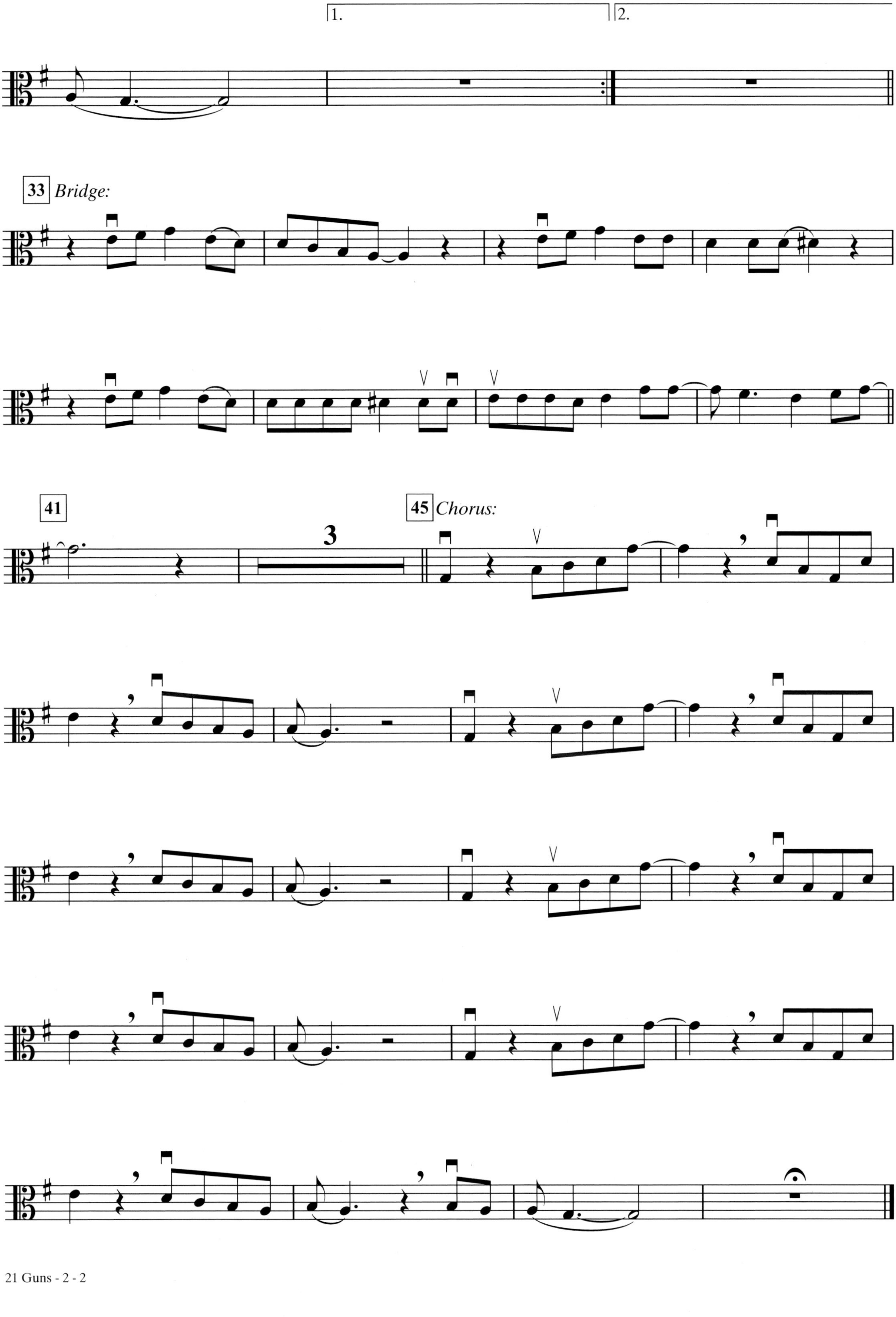
1.
2.
33 Bridge:
41
3
45 Chorus:

A WHITER SHADE OF PALE

Track 6: Demo
Track 7: Play-Along

Words and Music by
KEITH REID and GARY BROOKER

Moderately slow ♩ = 76

A Whiter Shade of Pale - 2 - 1

A Whiter Shade of Pale - 2 - 2

ALL I HAVE TO DO IS DREAM

Track 8: Demo
Track 9: Play-Along

Words and Music by
BOUDLEAUX BRYANT

Moderately (♩ = 104)

ANIMAL

Track 10: Demo
Track 11: Play-Along

Words and Music by
TIM PAGNOTTA, TYLER GLENN,
BRANDEN CAMPBELL, ELAINE DOTY
and CHRISTOPHER ALLEN

Animal - 3 - 1

BLUEBERRY HILL

Words and Music by
AL LEWIS, VINCENT ROSE
and LARRY STOCK

Moderately slow (♩. = 92)

BOTH SIDES, NOW

Track 14: Demo
Track 15: Play-Along

Words and Music by
JONI MITCHELL

BOULEVARD OF BROKEN DREAMS

Track 16: Demo
Track 17: Play-Along

Words by
BILLIE JOE

Music by
GREEN DAY

Boulevard of Broken Dreams - 2 - 1

DANCING QUEEN

Words and Music by
BENNY ANDERSSON, STIG ANDERSON
and BJORN ULVAEUS

Dancing Queen - 2 - 1

DESPERADO

Words and Music by
DON HENLEY and GLENN FREY

Desperado - 2 - 1

DON'T STOP BELIEVIN'

Words and Music by
JONATHAN CAIN, NEAL SCHON
and STEVE PERRY

Moderate rock (♩ = 120)

Don't Stop Believin' - 2 - 1

Don't Stop Believin' - 2 - 2

DOMINO

Words and Music by
CLAUDE KELLY, LUKASZ GOTTWALD,
MAX MARTIN, HENRY WALTER
and JESSICA CORNISH

Track 24: Demo
Track 25: Play-Along

Domino - 2 - 1

DYNAMITE

Words and Music by
BONNIE McKEE, TAIO CRUZ,
LUKASZ GOTTWALD, MAX MARTIN
and BENJAMIN LEVIN

Track 28: Demo
Track 29: Play-Along

EVERYBODY TALKS

Words and Music by
TYLER GLENN and TIM PAGNOTTA

Moderately fast rock (♩ = 152)

Everybody Talks - 3 - 1

Track 30: Demo
Track 31: Play-Along

FIREWORK

Words and Music by
KATY PERRY, MIKKEL ERIKSEN,
TOR ERIK HERMANSEN, SANDY WILHELM
and ESTER DEAN

Moderate rock (♩ = 126)

Firework - 2 - 1

FORGET YOU

Track 32: Demo
Track 33: Play-Along

Words and Music by
CHRISTOPHER BROWN, PETER HERNANDEZ,
ARI LEVINE, PHILIP LAWRENCE
and THOMAS CALLAWAY

Moderately bright soul (= 126)

Forget You - 2 - 1

GIMME SOME LOVIN'

Words and Music by
STEVE WINWOOD, MUFF WINWOOD
and SPENCER DAVIS

GO YOUR OWN WAY

Track 36: Demo
Track 37: Play-Along

Words and Music by
LINDSEY BUCKINGHAM

GOOD TIME

Words and Music by
MATTHEW THIESSEN, BRIAN LEE
and ADAM YOUNG

Moderate dance tempo (♩ = 120)

Good Time - 2 - 1

Track 40: Demo
Track 41: Play-Along

GRENADE

Words and Music by
CLAUDE KELLY, PETER HERNANDEZ,
BRODY BROWN, PHILIP LAWRENCE,
ARI LEVINE and ANDREW WYATT

Moderately slow (♩ = 112)

Grenade - 2 - 1

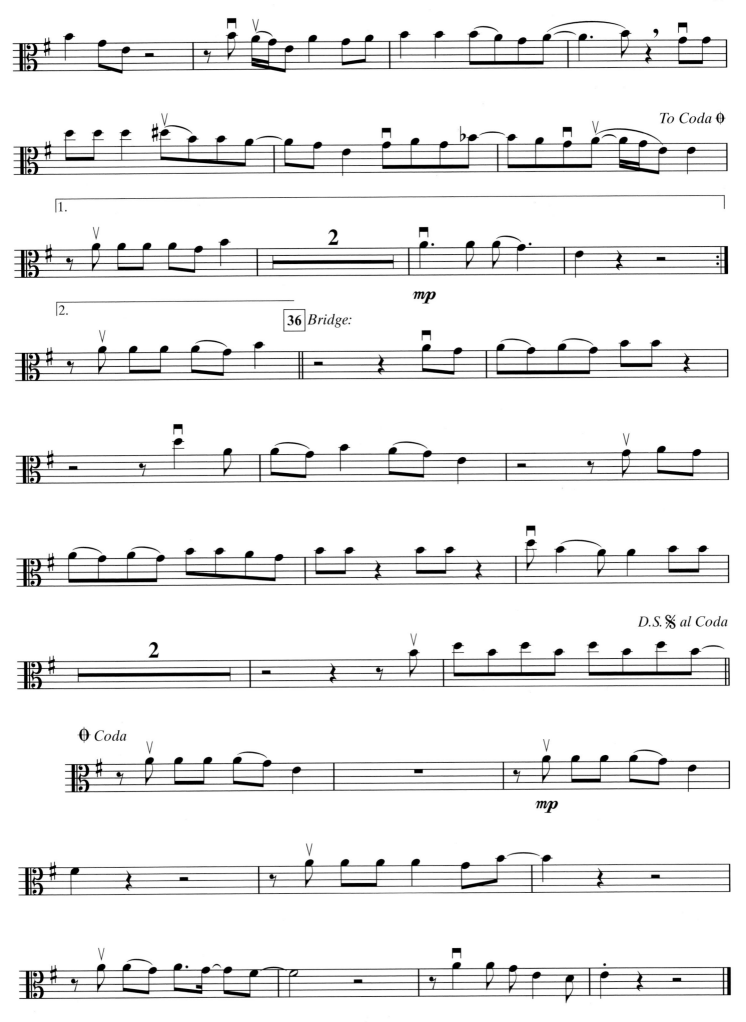

(YOUR LOVE KEEPS LIFTING ME)
HIGHER AND HIGHER

Track 42: Demo
Track 43: Play-Along

Words and Music by
GARY JACKSON, CARL SMITH
and RAYNARD MINER

Fast (♩ = 184)

10 *Verse:*

18

26 𝄋 *Chorus:*

(Your Love Keeps Lifting Me) Higher and Higher - 2 - 1

(Your Love Keeps Lifting Me) Higher and Higher - 2 - 2

Track 44: Demo
Track 45: Play-Along

HOME

Moderately (♩ = 120)

Words and Music by
DREW PEARSON and GREG HOLDEN

HONKY TONK WOMEN

Track 46: Demo
Track 47: Play-Along

Words and Music by
MICK JAGGER and KEITH RICHARDS

Moderate rock (♩ = 116)

* Percussion intro for accompaniment track.

HOTEL CALIFORNIA

Words and Music by
DON HENLEY, GLENN FREY
and DON FELDER

Hotel California - 3 - 1

HOW DEEP IS YOUR LOVE

Track 50: Demo
Track 51: Play-Along

Words and Music by
BARRY GIBB, MAURICE GIBB
and ROBIN GIBB

I ONLY HAVE EYES FOR YOU

Words by
AL DUBIN

Music by
HARRY WARREN

IN MY HEAD

Words and Music by
CLAUDE KELLY, JONATHAN ROTEM
and JASON DESROULEAUX

In My Head - 3 - 1

In My Head - 3 - 3

IN THE MIDNIGHT HOUR

Track 56: Demo
Track 57: Play-Along

Words by
WILSON PICKETT

Music by
STEVE CROPPER

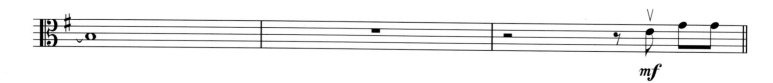

In the Midnight Hour - 2 - 1

In the Midnight Hour - 2 - 2

Track 58: Demo
Track 59: Play-Along

JAR OF HEARTS

Words and Music by
DREW LAWRENCE, CHRISTINA PERRI
and BARRETT YERETSIAN

Jar of Hearts - 3 - 1

53 *Chorus:*

mf

rall. *mp*

Track 60: Demo
Track 61: Play-Along

MOONDANCE

Words and Music by
VAN MORRISON

JUST A KISS

Words and Music by
CHARLES KELLEY, DAVE HAYWOOD,
HILLARY SCOTT and DALLAS DAVIDSON

Just a Kiss - 2 - 1

JUST THE WAY YOU ARE (AMAZING)

Track 64: Demo
Track 65: Play-Along

Words and Music by
KHALIL WALTON, PETER HERNANDEZ,
PHILIP LAWRENCE, ARI LEVINE
and KHARI CAIN

Moderately (♩ = 112)

Just the Way You Are (Amazing) - 2 - 1

Track 66: Demo
Track 67: Play-Along

MR. KNOW IT ALL

Words and Music by
BRETT JAMES, ESTER DEAN,
BRIAN KENNEDY and DANTE JONES

Moderate rock (♩ = 100)

Mr. Know It All - 2 - 1

Track 68: Demo
Track 69: Play-Along

NEED YOU NOW

Words and Music by
DAVE HAYWOOD, CHARLES KELLEY,
HILLARY SCOTT and JOSH KEAR

Moderately (♩ = 108)

Need You Now - 2 - 1

Track 70: Demo
Track 71: Play-Along

PART OF ME

Words and Music by
KATY PERRY, LUKASZ GOTTWALD,
MAX MARTIN and BONNIE McKEE

Medium dance tempo (♩ = 132)

Part of Me - 2 - 1

Track 72: Demo
Track 73: Play-Along

PAYPHONE

Words and Music by
WIZ KHALIFA, ADAM LEVINE,
BENJAMIN LEVIN, AMMAR MALIK,
JOHAN SCHUSTER and DANIEL OMELIO

Moderately (♩ = 120)

13 *Verse:*

Payphone - 2 - 1

(WE'RE GONNA)

ROCK AROUND THE CLOCK

Track 74: Demo
Track 75: Play-Along

Words and Music by
MAX C. FREEDMAN
and JIMMY DE KNIGHT

Moderately bright rock (♩ = 176)

(I CAN'T GET NO) SATISFACTION

Track 76: Demo
Track 77: Play-Along

Words and Music by
MICK JAGGER and KEITH RICHARDS

Moderately, driving (♩ = 132)

Track 78: Demo
Track 79: Play-Along

RHYTHM OF LOVE

Words and Music by
TIM LOPEZ

Rhythm of Love - 2 - 1

SMILE

Track 80: Demo
Track 81: Play-Along

Words and Music by
MATTHEW SHAFER, BLAIR DALY,
J.T. HARDING and JEREMY BOSE

Slow groove, half-time feel (♩ = 72) (♫ = ♪³♪)

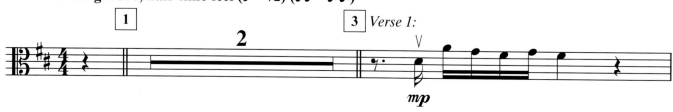

Smile - 2 - 1

SOUL MAN

Track 82: Demo
Track 83: Play-Along

Words and Music by
ISAAC HAYES and DAVID PORTER

SUNSHINE OF YOUR LOVE

Track 84: Demo
Track 85: Play-Along

Words and Music by
JACK BRUCE, PETE BROWN
and ERIC CLAPTON

Track 86: Demo
Track 87: Play-Along

SPIRIT IN THE SKY

Words and Music by
NORMAN GREENBAUM

Moderate blues shuffle (♩ = 128) (♫ = ♩³♪)

Spirit in the Sky - 2 - 1

THE PRAYER

Track 88: Demo
Track 89: Play-Along

Words and Music by
CAROLE BAYER SAGER and DAVID FOSTER

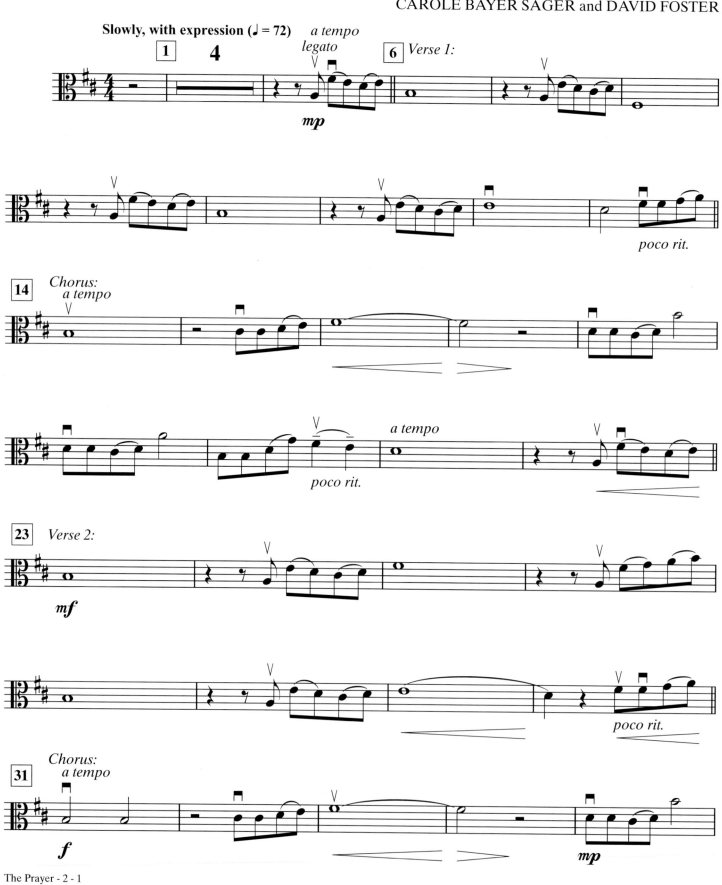

The Prayer - 2 - 1

The Prayer - 2 - 2

Track 90: Demo
Track 91: Play-Along

WE ARE YOUNG

Words and Music by
NATE RUESS, ANDREW DOST,
JACK ANTONOFF and JEFFREY BHASKER

We Are Young - 3 - 1

WHEN A MAN LOVES A WOMAN

Track 92: Demo
Track 93: Play-Along

Words and Music by
CALVIN LEWIS and ANDREW WRIGHT

WIDE AWAKE

Track 94: Demo
Track 95: Play-Along

Words and Music by
KATY PERRY, BONNIE McKEE,
LUKASZ GOTTWALD, MAX MARTIN
and HENRY WALTER

Wide Awake - 2 - 1

YOU RAISE ME UP

Words and Music by
ROLF LOVLAND and
BRENDAN GRAHAM

YOU SEND ME

Track 98: Demo
Track 99: Play-Along

Words and Music by
SAM COOKE

Harry Potter
INSTRUMENTAL SOLOS

Play-along with the best-known themes from the Harry Potter film series! The compatible arrangements are carefully edited for the Level 2–3 player, and include an accompaniment CD which features a demo track and play-along track.

Titles: Double Trouble • Family Portrait • Farewell to Dobby • Fawkes the Phoenix • Fireworks • Harry in Winter • Harry's Wondrous World • Hedwig's Theme • Hogwarts' Hymn • Hogwarts' March • Leaving Hogwarts • Lily's Theme • Obliviate • Statues • A Window to the Past • Wizard Wheezes.

(00-39211) | Flute Book & CD | $12.99
(00-39214) | Clarinet Book & CD | $12.99
(00-39217) | Alto Sax Book & CD | $12.99
(00-39220) | Tenor Sax Book & CD | $12.99
(00-39223) | Trumpet Book & CD | $12.99
(00-39226) | Horn in F Book & CD | $12.99
(00-39229) | Trombone Book & CD | $12.99
(00-39232) | Piano Acc. Book & CD | $18.99
(00-39235) | Violin Book & CD | $18.99
(00-39238) | Viola Book & CD | $18.99
(00-39241) | Cello Book & CD | $18.99